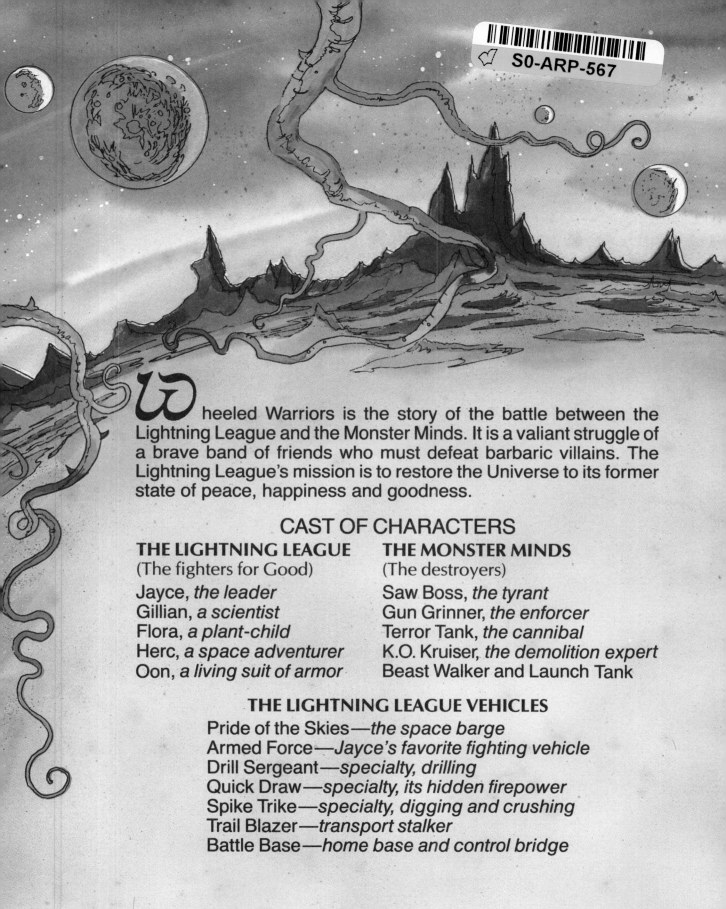

ⱳheeled Warriors is the story of the battle between the Lightning League and the Monster Minds. It is a valiant struggle of a brave band of friends who must defeat barbaric villains. The Lightning League's mission is to restore the Universe to its former state of peace, happiness and goodness.

CAST OF CHARACTERS

THE LIGHTNING LEAGUE
(The fighters for Good)

Jayce, *the leader*
Gillian, *a scientist*
Flora, *a plant-child*
Herc, *a space adventurer*
Oon, *a living suit of armor*

THE MONSTER MINDS
(The destroyers)

Saw Boss, *the tyrant*
Gun Grinner, *the enforcer*
Terror Tank, *the cannibal*
K.O. Kruiser, *the demolition expert*
Beast Walker and Launch Tank

THE LIGHTNING LEAGUE VEHICLES

Pride of the Skies—*the space barge*
Armed Force—*Jayce's favorite fighting vehicle*
Drill Sergeant—*specialty, drilling*
Quick Draw—*specialty, its hidden firepower*
Spike Trike—*specialty, digging and crushing*
Trail Blazer—*transport stalker*
Battle Base—*home base and control bridge*

WHEELED WARRIORS™

THE RESCUE SQUAD

A GOLDEN BOOK
Western Publishing Company, Inc.
Racine, Wisconsin 53404

Library of Congress Catalog Card Number: 85-070078
ISBN 0-307-16123-4

A B C D E F G H I J

During their quest to find Jayce's scientist father, the Lightning League visited many planets. The planet they had landed on had not yet been invaded by the Monster Minds.

"Perhaps," said Gillian, the wizard-like scientist, "we can stop those mutated plants from ever spoiling this world."

"How?" asked Jayce, leader of the Lightning League.

"There is only one way," replied Gillian.

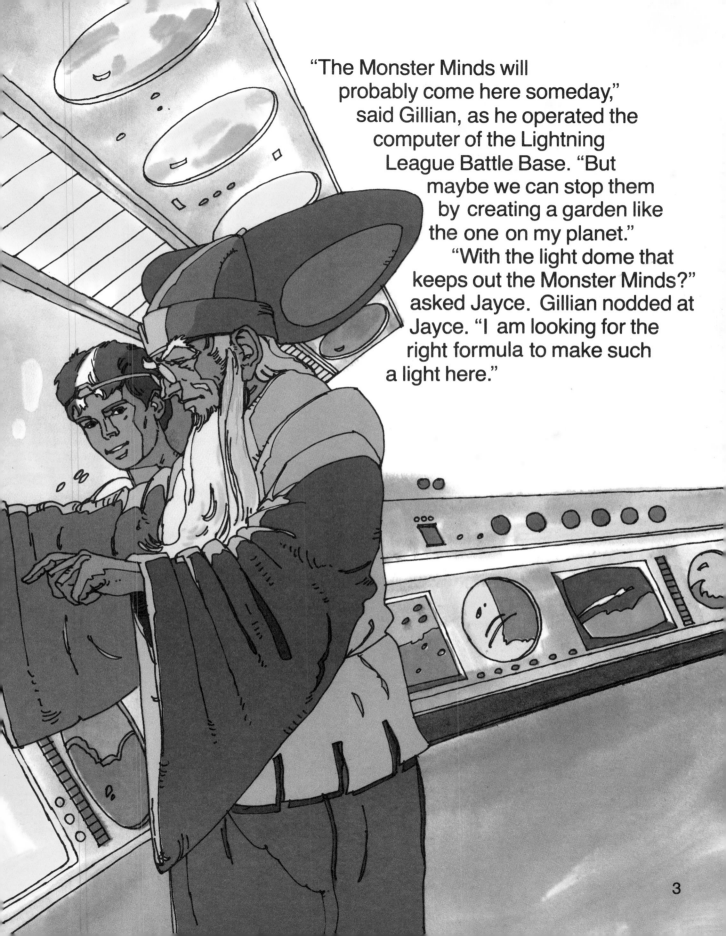

"The Monster Minds will probably come here someday," said Gillian, as he operated the computer of the Lightning League Battle Base. "But maybe we can stop them by creating a garden like the one on my planet."

"With the light dome that keeps out the Monster Minds?" asked Jayce. Gillian nodded at Jayce. "I am looking for the right formula to make such a light here."

While Gillian used the computers, Jayce thought of other ways to help this planet. He would use the Lightning League's machines and Gillian's robots to build a town for the people who would come to live here. The town would be strong enough to survive a Monster Minds' attack.

The Battle Base opened. Out rolled Armed Force, Spike Trike, Drill Sergeant and Quick Draw.

Jayce expertly drove Armed Force. This vehicle had been built by Gillian for Jayce's father. Now it belonged to Jayce. He used Armed Force's lasers to blast huge rock chunks from the mountainside.

Then, using the vehicle's arm, Jayce picked up the stones that would be used to make walls.

Jayce felt good, knowing that Armed Force was being used for something besides a battle vehicle.

Herc Stormsailor was captain of the Pride of the Skies, the space barge in which the Lightning League traveled. He drove the vehicle called Drill Sergeant. He used its drill to dig out gravel and stones.

The materials would be used to make streets in the new town.

As Herc operated Drill Sergeant's tools, he thought of the money he could be making if he were getting paid.

The robots that drove Quick Draw and Spike Trike were invented by Gillian. They did their work without question.

Quick Draw's front shield opened, showing its laser guns. The lasers neatly cut down trees which would become lumber for houses. Spike Trike, meanwhile, used its mighty wheel and cleared the spot where the new town would be built.

7

At that same time, something sinister was happening in space. Gigantic vines reached out through the void. They moved as if they had wills of their own.

Actually, *other* minds controlled the vines. Those minds made the vines twist and grow until they reached the planet where the Lightning League worked. These vines were under the control of the terrible Monster Minds!

The vines made a kind of highway through space. On these vines the Monster Minds traveled from their planet to other planets they hoped to conquer.

Saw Boss was the leader of the Monster Minds, and he planned to take over another world. Then that world's resources would be his. Its soil would grow many more of his kind. Speeding along with him were his henchmen Terror Tank, Gun Grinner and K.O. Kruiser.

While Jayce and his friends were busy, Flora and Oon were having fun. Flora had built a sand castle.

Oon tried to impress Flora with his past adventures. "Then there was the time I dashed into a castle, just like yours. I used my magic lance against a giant," he said. His metal visor clattered as he spoke.

"That's nice," said Flora with a smile.

"Ah, yes!" he went on. "Not even that giant could..."

Flora's attention was somewhere else. The girl, grown from a flower in Gillian's garden, was fascinated by the plants on this world. She smiled at one of the plants.

"Hi!" she said to the plant. But she spoke with her thoughts, not with her voice. "My name's Flora. Want to say something to me? I'd like to be your friend."

Flora touched the side of her head. She used her gift of telepathy, which let her sense what others were thinking.

The plant greeted her. Then, suddenly, it became afraid. It was picking up thoughts from somewhere else in the area. Flora felt the invading thoughts, too.

"What's wrong, Flora?" asked Oon.

Flora did not answer Oon. The roar of motors caused them to turn to see what was happening.

Four Monster Minds rolled out of hiding. "So," said Saw Boss, laughing, "what have we here? A fair maiden guarded by a brave knight?"

"We'll see how brave he is," said Terror Tank, "after I have his lance for lunch!"

"This knight won't protect anybody!" said K.O. Kruiser.

"Not even himself!" laughed Gun Grinner, aiming his ray guns.

"And if these two are on this planet," said Saw Boss, "they're not alone. My worst enemy Jayce must be here too, with the rest of the Lightning League! Now that's convenient."

"What'll we do with these two?" asked K.O. Kruiser.

"Capture them! And use them to get the others!"

14

Though not the bravest of heroes, Oon would never let harm come to Flora. "Keep back!" he said. He hoped that the lance's magic would protect them until they could escape.

Flora knew there was no magic in the lance. But she said nothing. And she admired Oon's display of bravery.

"The fool thinks he can stop us with that!" roared Saw Boss. "Let's show him that he's wrong!"

"Magic lance, stop those
ugly weeds!" said Oon. But the
lance did nothing. Oon's hands
shook. The lance dropped to
the ground. It started sliding
down the hillside. "Get on,
Flora! We're going for a ride!"

The ride down the hill was
shaky. But Flora trusted Oon.
She had no other choice.
"Where are we going?" she
asked. But Oon had no answer.

The lance took them down to the river. Both Flora and Oon were happy for the gentle splashdown.

"You see," said Oon, "the magic lance saved us."

"If only it had kept us dry!" said Flora.

But they were not completely safe. Above them, the Monster Minds looked down with anger. Scowls appeared on their ugly faces.

"Get them!" commanded Saw Boss.

"I'll take the lead!" said Terror Tank. He rolled ahead of the other Monster Minds. "I'm a natural hunter!"

Saw Boss saw the smile that appeared briefly on Terror Tank's face. He knew what the vehicle was doing. This was yet another try for him to prove he could be a leader. But Saw Boss was not worried.

"Follow Terror Tank," he said to the others, "for now."

After Oon pulled himself onto shore, he tossed the lance across the water to Flora. She climbed on it and used it as a bridge to get to where Oon stood.

"You saved my life, Oon," she said. "Thanks."

"You mean *we* did it, me and my 'magic' lance," Oon proudly boasted.

The Monster Minds were getting closer and closer. Saw Boss was laughing loudly, as he followed his companions.

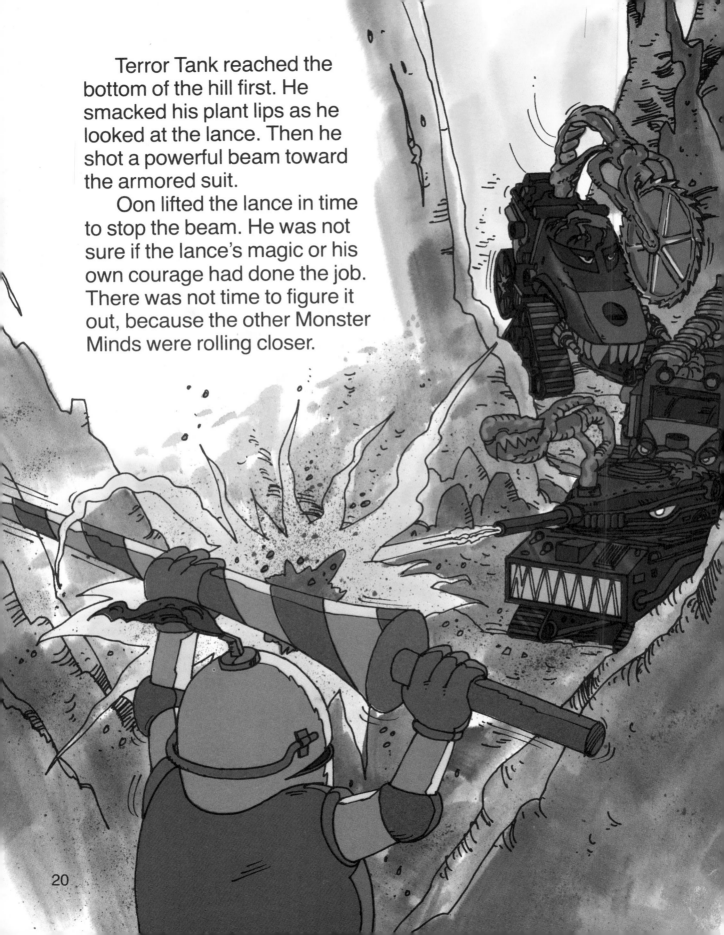

Terror Tank reached the bottom of the hill first. He smacked his plant lips as he looked at the lance. Then he shot a powerful beam toward the armored suit.

Oon lifted the lance in time to stop the beam. He was not sure if the lance's magic or his own courage had done the job. There was not time to figure it out, because the other Monster Minds were rolling closer.

For now, Oon thought the best thing to do was to get away. Taking Flora's hand, he ran through the woods, his armor clanking.

Something dark was ahead of them—a deep hole in the ground that could swallow them up. The lance slipped from Oon's grasp. It dropped across the hole, again making a fine bridge.

And still the Monster Minds chased after them.

Someone besides the Monster Minds was looking for Flora and Oon. This was Brock, the flying fish. Brock was another of Gillian's creations, a hybrid of fish and bird. He was devoted to Flora, and only she could communicate with him.

When Brock found that Flora was no longer playing where she had been, he flew off to find her. In his mind, he sensed a faint trace of her thoughts. She was somewhere nearby.

But Brock could not find Flora. He flew back to the Battle Base. There, the rest of the Lightning League were busy working on the new garden.

Brock whistled loudly, but no one could understand him.

"I am worried," said Gillian. "He seems to be upset."

"Has anyone seen Flora and Oon?" asked Jayce.

"Hey, maybe something's happened to them!" said Herc.

Because Flora might be in danger, Herc quit thinking
about not getting paid for his work. "Warm up Trail
Blazer," he said, "and let's get going."

Soon Trail Blazer, with Quick Draw aboard, rolled
down the ramp. Jayce drove and a worried Herc sat
beside him.

Gillian and the robots stayed near the Battle Base and
continued their work.

"Can't this thing go any faster?" grumbled Herc.

Jayce drove Trail Blazer at top speed. The Stalker sped over ground that would have slowed down other vehicles.

Maybe Jayce could not understand Brock's whistles, but he could follow the winged fish. He knew Brock could take them to the spot where he had picked up Flora's thoughts.

"He's doing it, Herc!" said Jayce. But for Brock the thoughts were getting fainter.

Flora and Oon fled through the woods. They were running farther away from the Battle Base. And they were getting tired. Behind them, the four Monster Minds were getting too close.

"Give Up!" said Gun Grinner. "You'll never get away on foot!"

"We'll never give up!" said Flora. "Will we, Oon?"

"Uh, *never* is a long time," Oon muttered to himself.

They came to another hill. "Oh, Oon," said Flora, looking up the hill, "we'll never get away now."

"What did I say about 'never'?" Oon replied. Taking a stance like a knight of old, Oon used his lance. But he used it like a tool, not a weapon. Oon pushed its tip into the ground. He worked loose some rocks. The rocks banged against others on their way down the hill. Oon had started a landslide!

The Monster Minds rolled up to the stone barrier made by the landslide. "Tear it down!" commanded Saw Boss. He switched on his mighty buzz saw. A moment later, sharp saw teeth sliced through some of the stone.

Terror Tank and Gun Grinner blasted the barrier with lasers. Instantly some of the rock turned to powder. At the same time, K.O. Kruiser smashed other rocks with his wrecking ball.

Looking down, Flora and Oon saw the Monster Minds continue the chase. It would not be long before the four monstrous vehicles reached them.

"We have to climb higher," said Oon. But he really did not know what to do next. "Maybe, just maybe, there'll be something up ahead that will save us."

But the higher they climbed, the hotter it got!

"Oh, no!" shouted Flora. "It's a volcano!"

There was no place to go but up! Below, the Monster Minds were making their bumpy way up the slope. In a few more minutes, they would reach their prey.

"They're trapped!" said Saw Boss with glee.

He seemed to be right. Behind them, Flora and Oon felt the heat from the volcano's crater.

The Monster Minds began their attack. A stray blast hit the edge of the volcano's rim. It began to crumble.

"We need a miracle . . . and now!" cried Oon.

"And I see a miracle!" exclaimed Flora.

Trail Blazer was roaring out of the woods.

Herc's sharp eyes spotted Flora and Oon. They were slipping back into the crater. "Keep the uglies busy!" he said to Jayce. "I'm bailing out!"

Risking laser fire, Herc bolted up the volcano's slope. The Monster Minds were too busy trying to stop Trail Blazer to bother with Herc. He ran up to the crater. But he was not fast enough. Flora and Oon fell!

But Flora and Oon were not lost—yet. Somehow, they grabbed the inner rim of the crater. They held desperately onto the rough stone.

"Hang on just a few seconds more!" shouted Herc. He grabbed the fallen lance. He needed no magic to make the lance do its job. "Grab the lance," he said. "I'll pull you out of that oven!"

With a mighty tug, Herc pulled his two friends out of the crater.

"Herc," said Flora, "you saved us!"

"We're not out of the frying pan yet!" he told her.

Herc led Flora and Oon down the slope. Powerful rays shot around them. Ducking, the three Lightning League members kept on running. Ahead of them was Trail Blazer.

As they reached the Stalker, Herc saw that Trail Blazer was losing the fight. As always, Jayce fought fairly, but the four Monster Minds really ganged up on him.

"Their brains!" said Herc. "Maybe that's how to stop these creeps for a while." He yelled for Flora and Oon to get into Trail Blazer. Then keeping away from the lasers, Herc jumped aboard K.O. Kruiser. It did not take Herc long to lift out the dull-witted brain!

The other Monster Minds saw what Herc had done. They rolled toward him, giving Flora and Oon time to get to Trail Blazer.

"Okay, gruesome threesome," said Herc without fear. "Zap me, and you zap this little goodie first!"

"Do not fire!" shouted Saw Boss. "K.O. Kruiser is too valuable a warrior to lose!" So, for now, the battle ended.

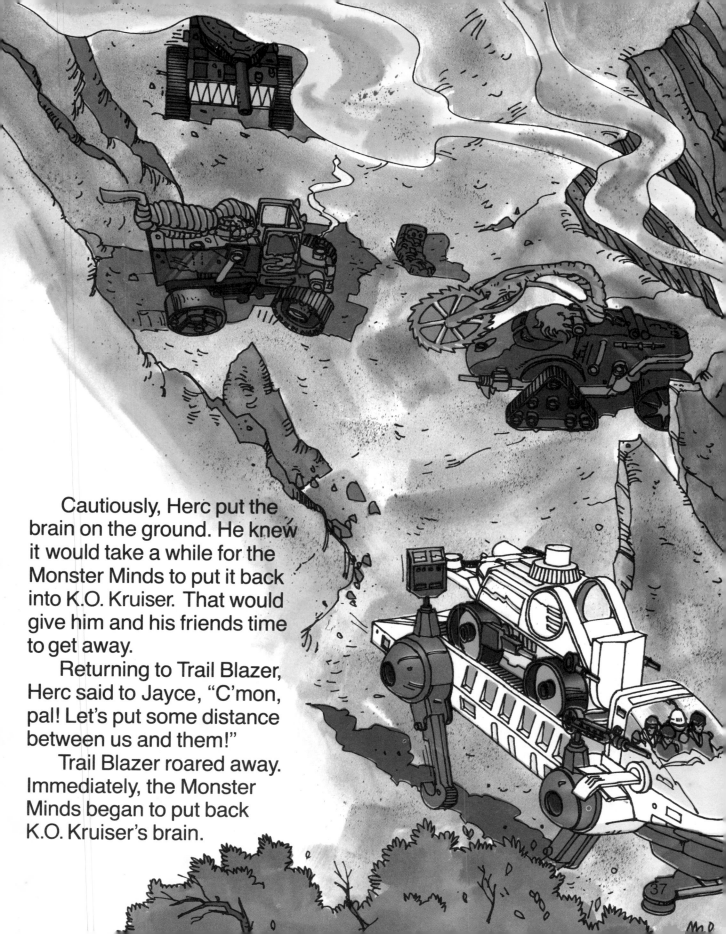

Cautiously, Herc put the
brain on the ground. He knew
it would take a while for the
Monster Minds to put it back
into K.O. Kruiser. That would
give him and his friends time
to get away.

Returning to Trail Blazer,
Herc said to Jayce, "C'mon,
pal! Let's put some distance
between us and them!"

Trail Blazer roared away.
Immediately, the Monster
Minds began to put back
K.O. Kruiser's brain.

By the time Trail Blazer returned to the Battle Base, Gillian was finishing his new garden. He and the robots had worked fast to get the work done. Soon the garden would be ready to become a home for anyone who needed a safe place in which to live.

"All we need to do is test the energy dome," Gillian said. "If it works, it will keep out the Monster Minds."

Gillian was about to get the chance to really test his invention. At that moment, Saw Boss was leading his warriors through the underbrush. K.O. Kruiser, his brain returned, was among them.

"Hurry!" yelled Saw Boss. "Don't let them escape!"

Trees fell and rocks shattered as the Monster Minds made their charge. The four plant vehicles seemed unstoppable.

The Monster Minds
sped toward the Battle Base.
For a moment, Saw Boss
grinned. This garden
would soon belong to him!
"*Now!*" said Gillian. He
saw the Monster Minds getting
close to the garden. He pulled
the switch that turned on the
dome of light. "Did I succeed?"
Gillian asked himself.

The light appeared.
Instantly it stopped the
invaders.

The work of the Lightning League was finished on this planet. Gillian programmed special robots to guard the garden for future inhabitants, and then the Battle Base rose on anti-gravity beams to join the orbiting space barge.

"Now we can continue our quest," said Jayce. "Remember..."

"I know," said Herc. And the others joined in to say: "'A Courageous Heart, A Righteous Quest!'"